The Wee Adventures of Shabu Shabu™

A thrilling tale
told in eight parts

Book 2
The Silk Route

By Michael Csokas and Kristina Thornton

Copyright 2014
Steam Powered Productions

www.shabusworld.com   www.facebook.com/theweeadventuresofshabushabu

To our loving parents and
endlessly supportive families.

We love you!

THE WEE ADVENTURES OF SHABU SHABU™ – BOOK 2 – THE SILK ROUTE

Copyright © 2014 by Steam Powered Productions Pte Ltd
ISBN:978-981-07-9149-0

For permission requests, write to the publisher, addressed
"Attention: Permissions Coordinator,"
at the address below.

Steam Powered Productions Pte Ltd
info@shabusworld.com
www.shabusworld.com
www.facebook.com/TheWeeAdventuresofShabuShabu

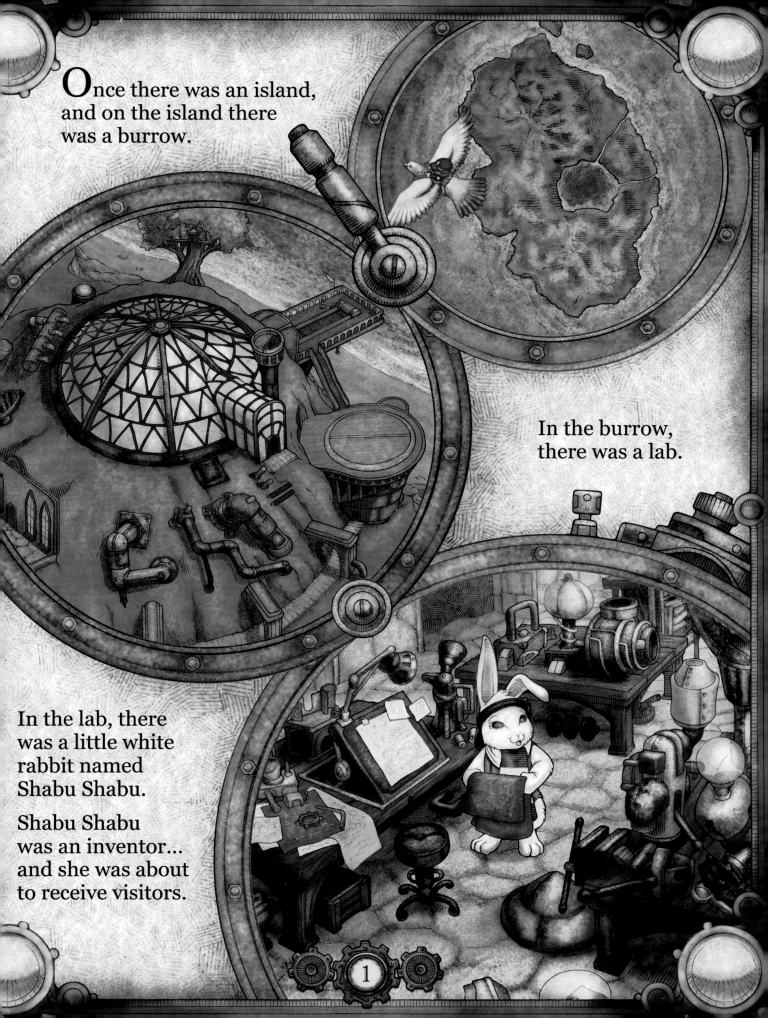

Once there was an island, and on the island there was a burrow.

In the burrow, there was a lab.

In the lab, there was a little white rabbit named Shabu Shabu.

Shabu Shabu was an inventor... and she was about to receive visitors.

Chow, what do you think about my test design for the new Lunar Venture Vessel?"

"Shabu, do we really need fifteen propellers and a Knotted Noodle Maker on a ship bound for the Moon?" said Chow.

Suddenly a cart crashed to a halt on the floor of the lab and several Messenger Mice tumbled out. They shakily got to their feet amongst the heap of scrolls that had fallen out with them.

"We really should fix that track," Shabu said.

"I would if I could find my wrench," said Chow.

"Halloo, Shabu! Halloo, Chow!" said little Mouse 227.

An old mouse cleared his throat and declared: "Messages for Ms. Shabu Shabu, delivered courtesy of the Department of Postal Affairs."

The mice bowed in unison. They straightened and held out scrolls to the rabbit.

3

Shabu read the messages an[d] frowned. "This is not good—n[o] good at all! No one is willing t[o] help provide materials for the new Lunar Venture Vessel. They say that a voyage to the Moon is dangerous nonsens[e]. I saw the Jade Rabbit wavin[g] at me through my telescope. It was an invitation—I'm sur[e] of it."

"You were sure about the Lon[g] Distance Breakfast Jam Launcher you built last week a[s] well, Fuzzy Brain, and I'm st[ill] cleaning jam out of my tail," the tinkering squirrel sniffe[d]. "It smells like grape."

"I will make the Launcher work, Noodle Head! And [I] will get to the Moon!"

The inventor's nose gave a twitch. "But first I need a balloon material strong enoug[h] to survive the journey."

4

Messenger Mouse 227 held out another scroll he had found under the cart. "There is one last message, Shabu." This scroll was different from the others, written on fine, sturdy silk instead of the usual stiff paper. Shabu read the letter and this time she smiled.

"Chow, read this."

His eyes skimmed the letter and then he said, "227, do you know who sent it?"

"No one saw the sender." The Mouse pulled out a map. "But I can tell you that the scroll was deposited at a drop station here." He pointed to a dot in a huge jungle that lay far across the ocean.

Shabu Rabbit,

We have learned of your quest and offer assistance. The scroll you hold is made from an unusually special material—silk able to survive the most terrible cold and the most fiery heat. With certainty it will suit your needs. Come to where this message was sent and you will receive what you desire.

Under the Moon,
Sky and
Stars Above,

The Messenger Mice excused themselves from the burrow and left Shabu to ponder the mysterious letter.

"There must be some way to identify this claw mark!"

"Let's check your grandfather's Jade Workshop. We can use the Pictoprojector to hunt for information!"

The two friends raced down the hidden spiral staircase to the secret workshop and were soon placing slides into the illuminated machine.

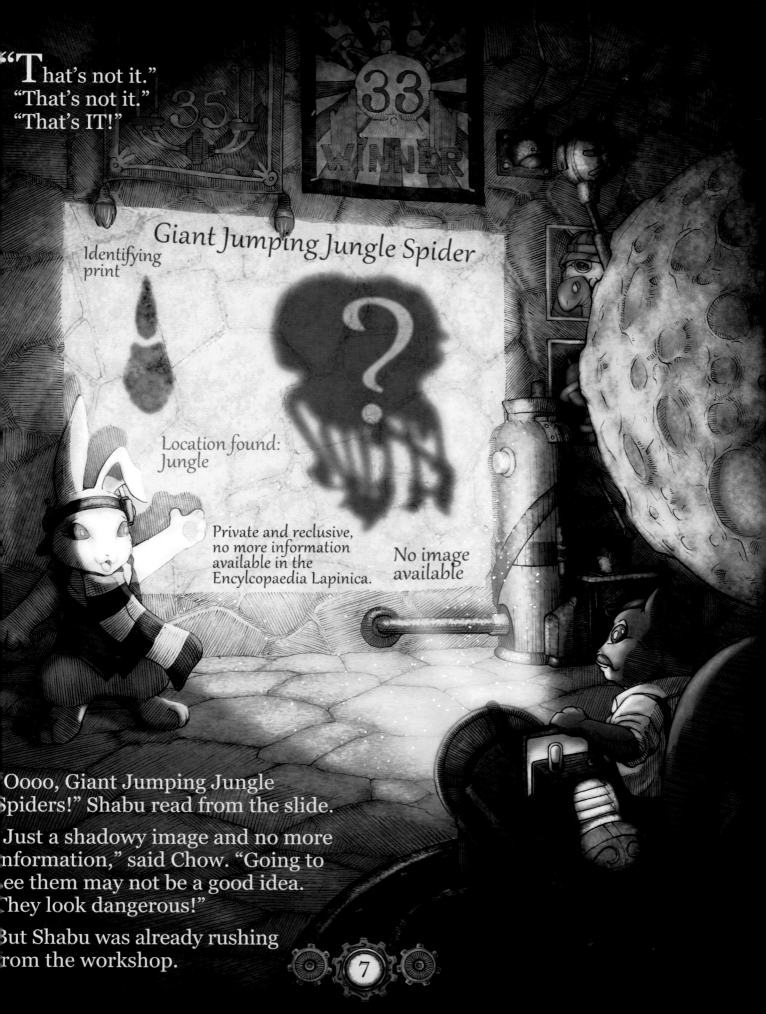

"**T**hat's not it."
"That's not it."
"That's IT!"

Giant Jumping Jungle Spider

Identifying
print

?

Location found:
Jungle

Private and reclusive,
no more information
available in the
Encylcopaedia Lapinica.

No image
available

"Oooo, Giant Jumping Jungle
Spiders!" Shabu read from the slide.

"Just a shadowy image and no more
information," said Chow. "Going to
see them may not be a good idea.
They look dangerous!"

"But Shabu was already rushing
from the workshop.

"**W**hat are you doing, Fuzzy Brain?" Chow scampered behind her.

"Packing, Chow! There's no time to lose! Are the repairs completed on the old Venture Vessel?"

"You're leaving NOW? You have no plan and Grandfather's old hot air balloon isn't ready, especially for a trip that far. Also, Shabu you know I told my sister that I was leaving to visit her and her new kits."

"You mean you aren't coming with me?"

"I promised, Shabu. If you could just wait until I get back..."

Shabu stopped and gave the squirrel a determined look. "Chow, I can't wait. I will not spend another minute here when there is a chance I can get closer to reaching the Moon and the Jade Rabbit." She sighed. "You have a promise to keep but I have to go get that silk, Noodle Head. Please understand."

"I do, Fuzzy Brain. But it's still not safe to go without being prepared." Chow pulled a screwdriver from his apron. "I'll do what I can to get the old Venture Vessel ready for you. The last thing you need is to crash... again."

The balloon was quickly packed and after some repairs it waited at the air dock. Shabu looked at her friend. "Don't worry, Chow, I'll be back before you know it."

"But I'm not sure it's safUMPH—"

Shabu squeezed her best friend in a big hug. Then she jumped into the basket and hit the Vortex Biburner. Chow waved and tried to smile as the old Venture Vessel rose high into the sky.

"Say hello to Mama Mien, your sister and the kits for me, and don't forget to feed the Cantankerous Carnivorous Hibiscus!" she cried. Chow's brave grin became a cringe.

"I'm off to the jungle! Now, how am I going to get there?" She pulled out her map and plotted her course.

Desert Desert

Murky Jungle of Mur

Capering Coast

40.6

40.5

.5

Some Cranes were surprised to see a Rabbit flying!

Scruffy Mountains

Laughing Forest

A friendly Whale was in need of help! She somehow got an oar lodged in her baleen.

24

The Lesser Sea of Saw

10

Had a cup of seaweed tea with an old friend of Grandfather's, Professor Michio Tako.

42.6

43.6

Saw a strange ship travelling through the clouds with the Venture Vessel Spyscope. I've never seen anything like it.

It's the first time I've seen the Viking Lemmings looking for the edge of the world. They didn't want to stop and chat!

Isles of Land

4

43.5

THE BURROW

Lapin Island

Palm Hills

N

The ocean crossing was complete and Shabu's hot air balloon floated over the lush jungle. The rabbit scribbled notes in her journal.

Journal Entry 3

At last, the adventure I have been waiting for is here. This is thrilling! I belong out here. Being an adventurer must run in the family. Grandfather wanted me to stay in the burrow until I was ready, but ready for what—the Jade Rabbit or something else? The balloon has had a few problems but they were easily fixed in flight. Chow was worried for nothing. I suppose he only wants to make sure that I'm safe, just like everyone else.

I am drifting over the jungle canopy in the trusty old Venture Vessel. All I need to do is to find the spiders, collect the silk, and fly home to start building the new ship. I'll be back to the Burrow in no time.

The creaky Venture Vessel gave a jolt and suddenly veered off course. "What could be the problem now?"

P ulling levers and spinning valve wheels, Shabu did her best to regain control. But there was nothing she could do as the balloon plummeted toward the ground.

The balloon crashed through the trees and onto the jungle floor below. The basket tipped onto its side and Shabu spilled out in a pile of gadgets.

"This must be how the Messenge[r] Mice feel," mumbled the rabbit. She pulled herself clear of the wrecked balloon and wiped mu[d] off her cheeks.

"Well, that was better than the

Shabu examined her surroundings.

"These leaves are bigger than my body! And those trees must be hundreds of rabbits high. What are all those smells? And what's that low growling noise in the bushes?"

"YEEK!"

Without a moment to spare, Shabu threw herself from the path of an enormous tiger that burst from the trees. She sprang away as fast as she could, leaves whipping past her face, until she slid to a halt at the edge of a hidden waterfall that plunged into mist far below.

The tiger was right behind her and she had nowhere else to go. Shabu took a deep breath and jumped.

Blink, blink. "Ouch! That hurts! What happened?"

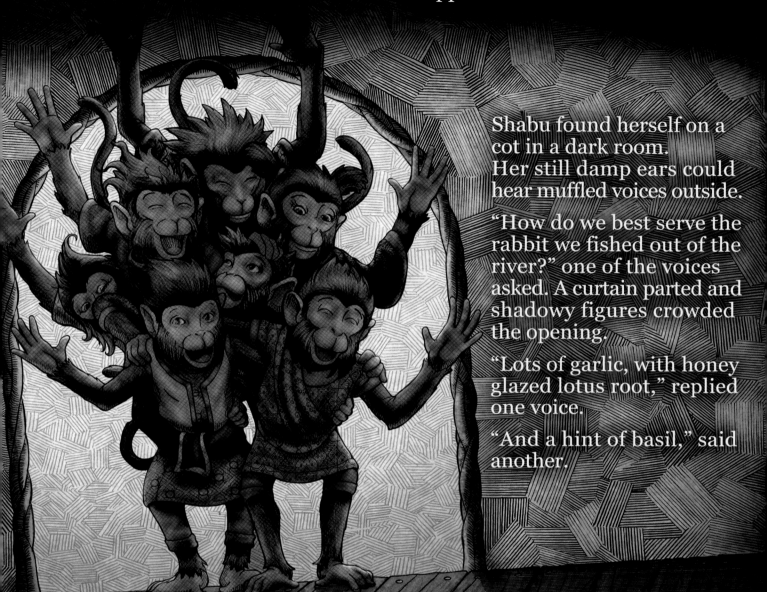

Shabu found herself on a cot in a dark room. Her still damp ears could hear muffled voices outside.

"How do we best serve the rabbit we fished out of the river?" one of the voices asked. A curtain parted and shadowy figures crowded the opening.

"Lots of garlic, with honey glazed lotus root," replied one voice.

"And a hint of basil," said another.

Shabu shot to her aching feet and squeaked, "My name is Shabu Shabu and I am not here to be served for lunch!"

Shadowy hands threw the curtains open wide, spilling light into the room. At the door stood grinning monkeys dressed in colorful silk clothing.

"We fooled you! We're not going to eat you!" the crowd cried out. "We beg your pardon, rabbit!"

One by one the monkeys placed strange fruits and trinkets at Shabu's feet and then rushed from the room laughing. A single monkey stayed behind. On his head he wore a golden crown topped with pearls.

The monkey smiled wide. "I am King Ka Shoo, son of Ah Shoo, leader of the Fisher Monkeys. I bid you welcome to this village. Did you enjoy our little joke?"

Shabu's fear changed to confusion and then anger. "That was a joke?" Shabu's nose began to twitch. "It was certainly not funny!"

The smile left the king's face. "You were not amused? Many, many pardons, young rabbit. But this is our way. We follow every joke with a gift and an apology because we must show respect. It is a lesson we learned long ago. We meant no harm."

Shabu's nose stopped twitching. "That's still an odd way to welcome a guest, but I accept your apology, King Ka Shoo."

"Splendid, Shabubu! Now let me show you our village."

"Why have you come to the jungle, Shabubu?" asked the monkey.

"To find the Giant Jumping Jungle Spiders, King Ka Shoo. They have something I need urgently. Could you help me find them as soon as possible?"

The king frowned. "Listen well, little one. You were just nearly eaten by the terrible tiger which has been terrorizing our village for ages."

Shabu trembled again at the memory of the terrifying beast.

The king went on.

"The spiders are far more dangerous. You must find another way to get what you need. As you are a newfound friend to the monkeys, this evening we will hold a performance in your honor. But for your own safety I insist that you return home in the morning."

Still thinking of the tiger, Shabu said in a small voice, "I'll consider it."

"The matter is settled. We will bring your flying ship back to the village. In the meantime, explore and see how we live."

Shabu walked down to the village but couldn't help but listen for the tiger's growl.

"Maybe what the king said is true. Maybe the jungle is too dangerous for a little rabbit like me," she said to herself. A terrible feeling of doubt washed over her.

"SHAboo, ShaBOOBOO, come and play with us!" A group of monkeys were playing a game with pearls by the river. Shabu's curiosity got the better of her and for the moment she forgot her fear.

"Where did you get these?" Shabu asked, eyeing one of their pearls with the Closerscope from her rucksack.

Here!" said a tiny monkey, and he dove into the water. A moment later he swam to the surface. Shee?" he said, a large earl between his teeth.

So that's why you're alled the Fisher Monkeys!"

The inventor walked along the river and watched as the villagers swayed back and forth on boats and chanted. Between each verse, they dove into the river and came back with pearls to put inside baskets.

"At a table of pearls when Moon is high,
An arrow to guide you—your time is nigh.

Above the ground a totem may be,
A key to the past only monkeys may see.

Once friends we were, that much is true.
Trust the stone monkey—in his prank a clue.

From hands that help, a shadow at noon,
A path to follow to find your boon."

"You have a fascinating chant, but what does it mean?" Shabu asked a giggling monkey.

The monkey shrugged his shoulders. "We have no idea. It's tradition!"

"But what if..."
The thought was left unfinished by another prank.

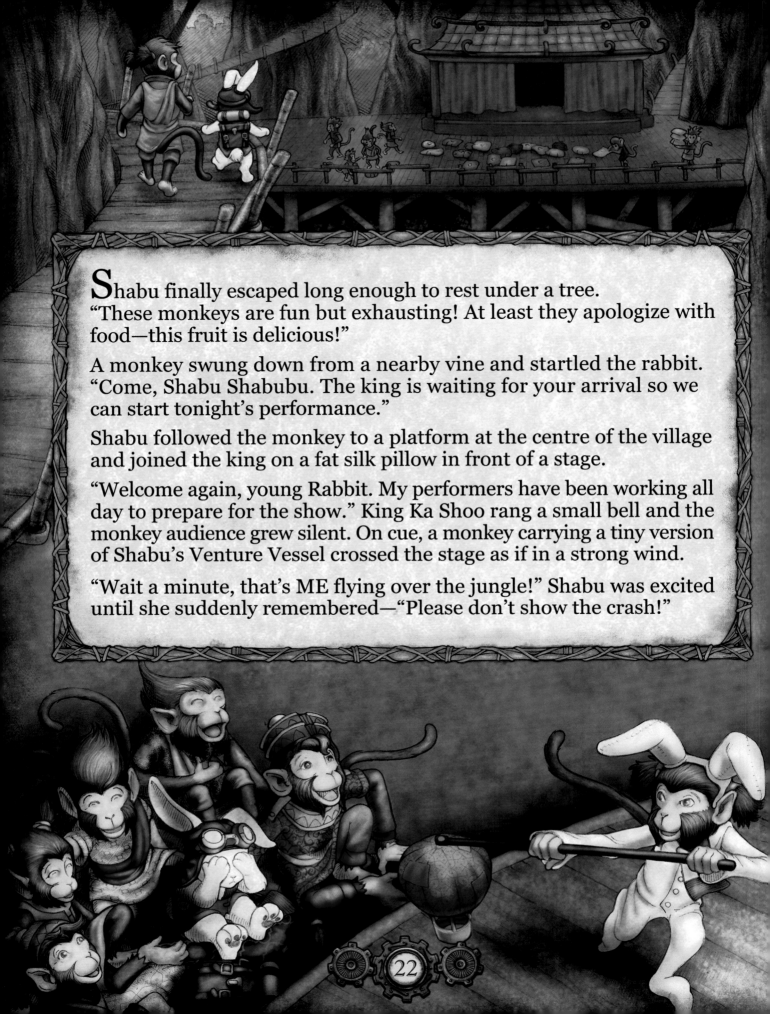

Shabu finally escaped long enough to rest under a tree. "These monkeys are fun but exhausting! At least they apologize with food—this fruit is delicious!"

A monkey swung down from a nearby vine and startled the rabbit. "Come, Shabu Shabubu. The king is waiting for your arrival so we can start tonight's performance."

Shabu followed the monkey to a platform at the centre of the village and joined the king on a fat silk pillow in front of a stage.

"Welcome again, young Rabbit. My performers have been working all day to prepare for the show." King Ka Shoo rang a small bell and the monkey audience grew silent. On cue, a monkey carrying a tiny version of Shabu's Venture Vessel crossed the stage as if in a strong wind.

"Wait a minute, that's ME flying over the jungle!" Shabu was excited until she suddenly remembered—"Please don't show the crash!"

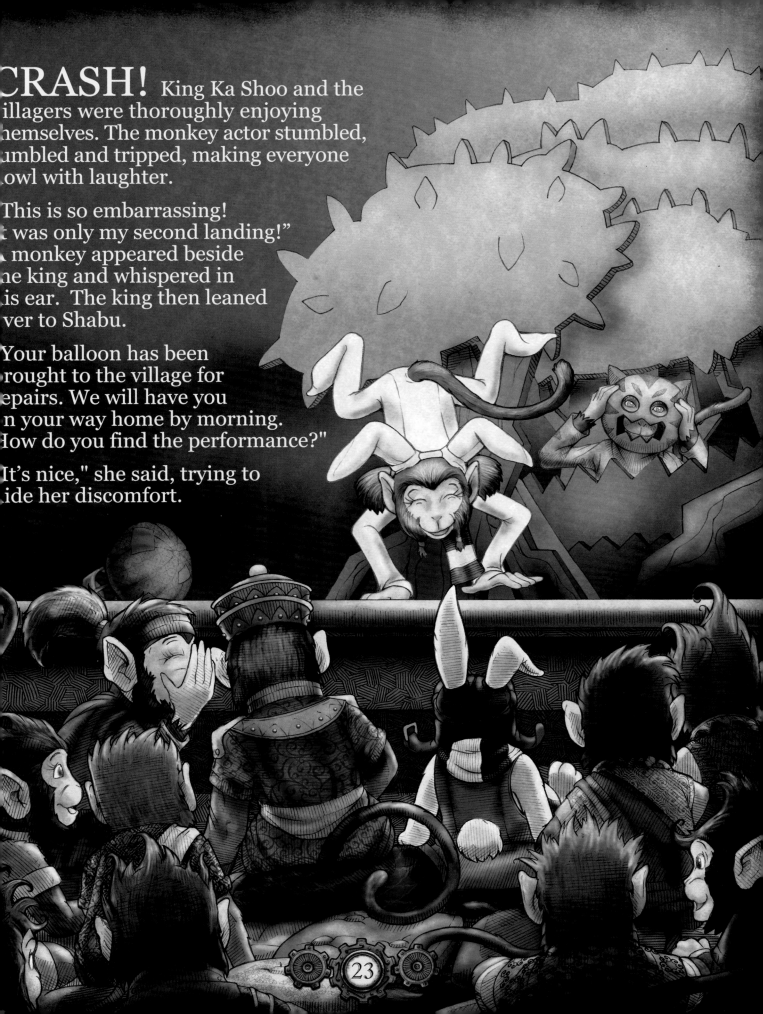

CRASH! King Ka Shoo and the villagers were thoroughly enjoying themselves. The monkey actor stumbled, tumbled and tripped, making everyone howl with laughter.

"This is so embarrassing! It was only my second landing!" A monkey appeared beside the king and whispered in his ear. The king then leaned over to Shabu.

"Your balloon has been brought to the village for repairs. We will have you on your way home by morning. How do you find the performance?"

"It's nice," she said, trying to hide her discomfort.

Shabu's eyes were glued to the stage.

"That's when that horrible brute chased me over the waterfall."

She shivered as she watched. Then a group of monkeys chased away the tiger and carried the rabbit out of the river. Finally, a single monkey walked to the front of the stage and declared, "The monkeys have saved the day. Let the savage tiger beware!" and he took a deep bow.

A low growl rumbled above the stage.

"Is that part of the play?" Shabu wondered aloud.

The monkeys all laughed at the sound and chattered for more, until the real tiger dropped from the shadows and landed squarely on the stage. The crowd froze. The tiger threw back his head and gave a great ROAR!

"Not again!" Terrified, Shabu jumped to her feet but was knocked off the platform by a wave of shrieking, fleeing villagers.

24

Shabu fell hard on the muddy ground beneath the stilted buildings. The sound of a heavy THUMP in the darkness nearby made her ears tremble.

"He's following me," thought Shabu. Twisting, she reached to find an invention that could get her back up to the safety of the higher levels.

"Oh, no! My rucksack is still on the platform!"

Her heart pounded in her ears as she scrambled to hide. Above her she could see shadows of panicked monkeys jumping back and forth through the gaps between the buildings. Shabu peeked around the corner of her hiding place. A huge shadow was making its way slowly and quietly through the forest of stilts. Shabu held her breath as she watched. The tiger came closer and closer, and then, he stalked right past her.

"Where is he going?" Shabu craned her neck to see.

A group of tiny monkeys that had fallen off the platform in the panic huddled in the mud directly in the path of the tiger. They whimpered softly, unaware of the shadowy beast behind them. Not far away Shabu saw a dark bundle of cloth—"It's the Venture Vessel!" Her eyes darted back and forth from the babies to her balloon. The tiger crept nearer to the monkeys. Gathering all her strength, the young inventor dashed straight towards the balloon.

With golden eyes fixed on the frightened monkeys, the tiger readied himself to pounce.

"YOOHALOOO! Look over here, you big meany!"

The tiger turned his head and from the Venture Vessel came the loud rumble of the Vortex Biburner and a flare of intense light.

Stunned, the tiger stumbled and bellowed. Shabu streaked across the muddy ground, right past the dazed beast.

"I've got you!" she shouted, grabbing the monkeys and pulling them close. She threw a grapple she had taken from the balloon and it hooked onto the platform above. They raced up the rope while below in the dark, the tiger roared furiously.

27

"King Ka Shoo, the tiger is right behind us!" The king heard Shabu's warning and called to the monkey actor dressed as Shabu.

As soon as the tiger clawed his way back up to the platform, the actor jumped directly in front of the tiger and stuck her tongue out. She bounced away and the beast followed into the shadows.

King Ka Shoo rushed to the inventor and the tiny monkeys jumped into his arms. "Are you harmed, Shabu Shabu?" the king asked.

"You called me by my real name! And no, I am not harmed." For the first time that day, all feeling of doubt left Shabu. "King Ka Shoo, I have decided not to go home without seeing the spiders." She stared up at the king with her nose twitching violently. "And there is a tiger who needs to be taught a very serious lesson."

The king was surprised by the change in the inventor. "There is something that I need to tell you about us monkeys and the spiders, my friend, but that can wait. For now," King Ka Shoo stared back at the rabbit, "What you say about the tiger is true; he has been a menace for far too long. What do you suggest?"

Shabu's eyes narrowed. "Oh, I have a few ideas."

Together Shabu and King Ka Shoo worked on a plan and soon every monkey in the village was busy. On the second day a monkey came from the jungle to report: "The tiger is still chasing our decoys, Your Majesty."

"You can call them back," said King Ka Shoo.

"We're ready," said Shabu.

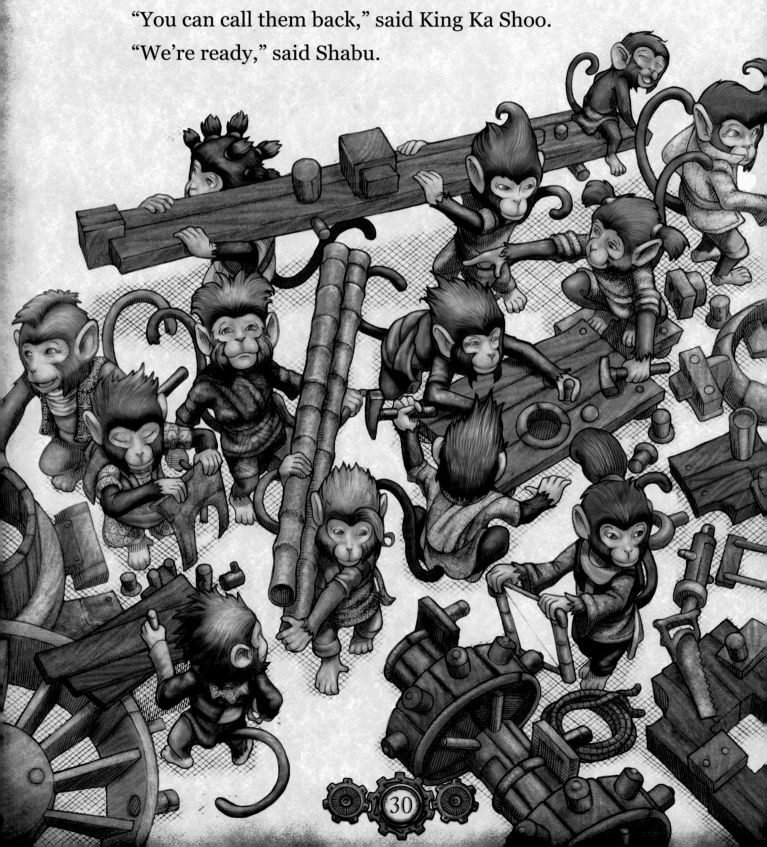

F ar in the jungle the tiger rested.

A cool breeze passed over him and a most delicious smell tickled his nose. He lifted his head high—it was coming from the monkey village. Taking a deep breath, he stood up and bounded into the jungle.

His mouth watered at the thought of eating something that smelled this good. What could it be?

Looking down on the monkey village, the tiger saw a large pot steaming on the stage where he had caused chaos days before.

The pot was being stirred by none other than the juicy rabbit that had escaped over the waterfall. Unable to wait any longer, his powerful legs tensed and with a growl the tiger leapt at the rabbit and her delicious dinner.

Sproing, KAPOW!

A hidden door under the stage gave way. The rabbit easily hopped to safety but the tiger and the steaming pot plunged into darkness under the village.

The monkeys taught
the bully a lesson.

The monkeys had a lot of lessons to teach.

The tiger landed in the basket of the Caterwauling Catapult with a grunt and a groan. Shabu took her place at a lever and the king addressed the tiger on behalf of the assembled monkeys.

"Dastardly tiger, you are unwelcome in this jungle. Never return!" Shabu tugged on the lever. "Oh, no! The lever is stuck! He's going to escape!"

The cringing tiger opened one eye.

"We are doomed!" cried the monkeys.

"Fooled you!" Shabu pulled the lever again. This time it came down with a satisfying KAPING and sent the tiger far away above the treetops. "I beg your pardon!" shouted the gleeful bunny. The crowd burst into noisy cheers and she passed out fruit to the villagers.

The king pulled Shabu away from the cheering crowd. "I promised to explain about the monkeys and spiders. Now is the time." It was King Ka Shoo's turn to be embarrassed.

Shabu looked up at the king. "The Giant Jumping Jungle Spiders are not dangerous, are they?"

The king's shoulders slumped. "Perhaps, perhaps not Shabu. When last our tribes were together, the spiders were very angry."

"Long ago, monkeys and spiders lived together in harmony. The spiders offered us knowledge and we taught the spiders how to laugh. They loved our fun until a young prince of the monkeys played a prank on the Spider King. The monkeys all laughed, thinking it was the funniest of jokes. The leader of the spiders was furious and demanded an apology. The Monkeys, only seeing the fun, refused. Our tribe was banished from the Grand Web, the home that we had shared."

"After wandering the jungle for a home, we built the village that you see here. The two leaders were very sad that there could be no understanding to keep the tribes together. But to make sure that we do not entirely forget each other, we fish for pearls and leave them at what we call the Sharing Table. The spiders take the pearls and leave silk in return. With it we weave cloth for sails, beautiful tapestries and our fine clothing. Though we trade, the two tribes have not spoken to or seen each other for many generations."

"Why do you not apologize to the spiders? The monkeys have learned their lesson," said the rabbit.

"I would, my friend, but the way to the Grand Web is lost."

Shabu put a paw to her chin. "I had a thought about this, King Ka Shoo. Please take me to the Sharing Table."

The king commanded a group of monkeys to bring torches and off they went.

After a long walk through the moonlit jungle they arrived at the Sharing Table.

"King Ka Shoo, look at this!" The rabbit pressed a button on her rucksack and a brass arm folded out with a lantern on the end.

"Your chant is more than it seems," Shabu said as she put a paw on the surface inlaid with pearls.

"What do you mean? We have used this chant for as long as the monkeys can remember."

The adventurer pointed toward a deep red pearl and then six more making a long arrow. "*At a table of pearls...*" Shabu started. "Don't you see? The chant gives directions back to the Grand Web and this is where we begin."

Early the next morning Shabu, King Ka Shoo and a small band of monkeys set off with great excitement in the direction of the red pearl arrow.
They chanted as they walked:

"At a table of pearls
when Moon is high,
An arrow to guide you—
your time is nigh."

Above the ground
a totem may be,
A key to the past
only monkeys may see.

Once friends we were,
that much is true.
Trust the stone monkey—
in his prank a clue."

"These hands that help,
a shadow at noon,
A path to follow
to find your boon...

Through pillars of stone,
seek your way home.
The star, the pearl,
this way you roam.

From horns of plenty,
one, three, five, four.
Follow the echoes
to stand at the door.

Pearls and silk,
in this we are bound.
At our beginning,
old friends are found."

The troupe pushed their way through the thick, green plants until they found themselves suddenly at the edge of a massive crater.

An ancient woven bridge spanned the distance to an enormous spindled tower rising from the centre.

The King of the Fisher Monkeys whispered, "Here at last."

41

"It doesn't look like a very strong bridge, my king. I'll go first," said one of the monkeys.

"No, I will go first," said the king, straightening his crown. He took a careful step onto the long, swaying bridge and then another. Seeing that the bridge was much stronger than it looked, the rest of the monkeys nervously followed as King Ka Shoo led the way to the tower.

The bridge ended at a huge archway of fine webs. The king stopped before entering and turned to Shabu. A hint of doubt showed on his face.

"Many thanks for returning us to the Grand Web, Shabu. My ancestors were never able to reach this dream, though I wonder," he hesitated, "if the spiders are still angry with us."

"You said the Monkey Tribe learned a lesson about respect long ago. After all this time, you can show them what you have learned. Just apologize."

King Ka Shoo, still worried, offered the little traveler a small smile. "No matter what happens, I am glad you crashed your balloon in our jungle."

Shabu laughed and grinned. "So am I, King Ka Shoo."

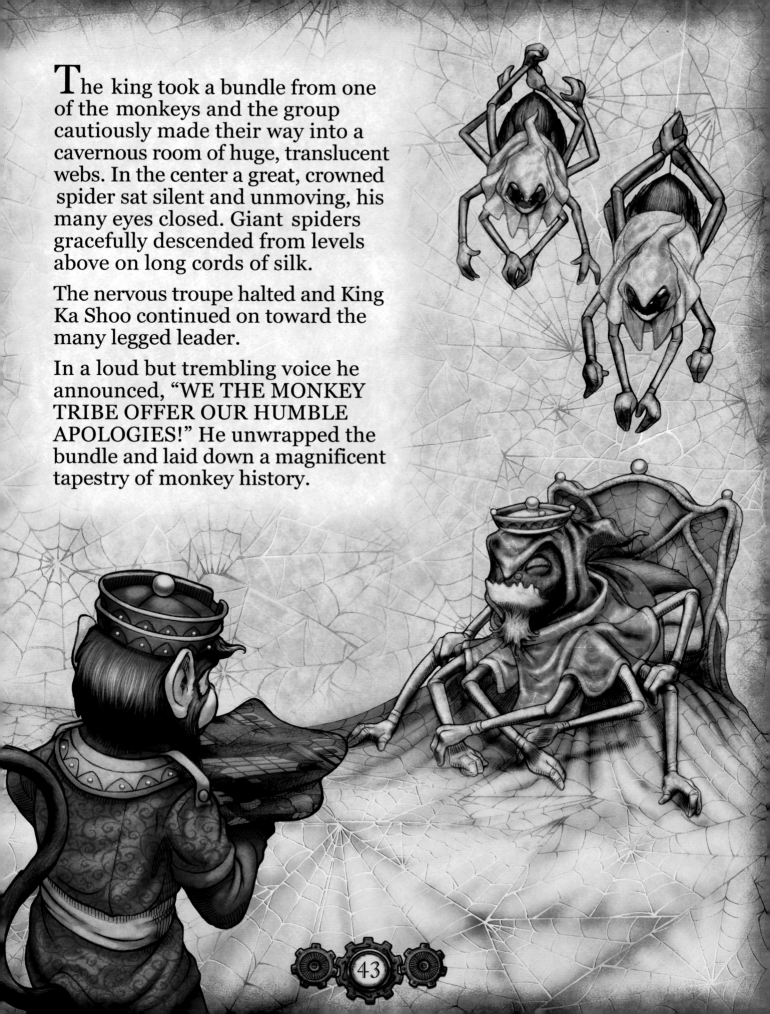

The king took a bundle from one of the monkeys and the group cautiously made their way into a cavernous room of huge, translucent webs. In the center a great, crowned spider sat silent and unmoving, his many eyes closed. Giant spiders gracefully descended from levels above on long cords of silk.

The nervous troupe halted and King Ka Shoo continued on toward the many legged leader.

In a loud but trembling voice he announced, "WE THE MONKEY TRIBE OFFER OUR HUMBLE APOLOGIES!" He unwrapped the bundle and laid down a magnificent tapestry of monkey history.

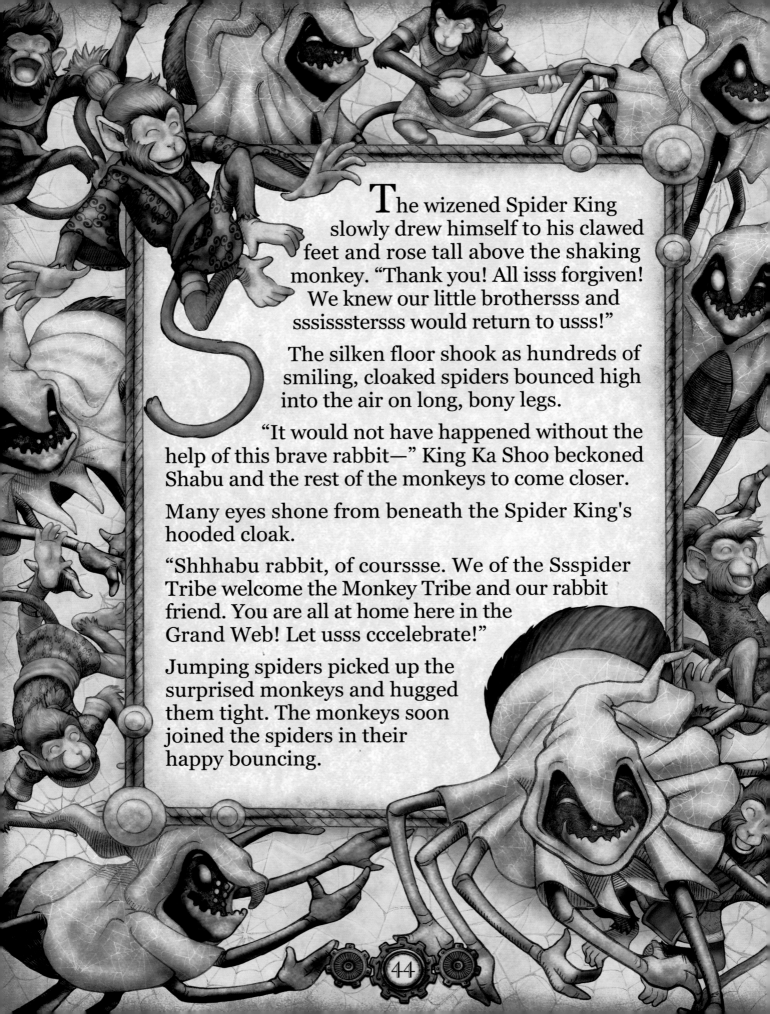

The wizened Spider King slowly drew himself to his clawed feet and rose tall above the shaking monkey. "Thank you! All isss forgiven! We knew our little brothersss and sssisssstersss would return to usss!"

The silken floor shook as hundreds of smiling, cloaked spiders bounced high into the air on long, bony legs.

"It would not have happened without the help of this brave rabbit—" King Ka Shoo beckoned Shabu and the rest of the monkeys to come closer.

Many eyes shone from beneath the Spider King's hooded cloak.

"Shhhabu rabbit, of courssse. We of the Ssspider Tribe welcome the Monkey Tribe and our rabbit friend. You are all at home here in the Grand Web! Let usss cccelebrate!"

Jumping spiders picked up the surprised monkeys and hugged them tight. The monkeys soon joined the spiders in their happy bouncing.

The party lasted long into the night. Finally the rabbit adventurer and the two kings found an opportunity to sit and talk.

"King of the Spiders, your tribe has collected pearls from the monkeys for so many years. But what are they for?"

The Spider King gestured up. In the ceiling of the web, far above their heads, thousands upon thousands of pearls glinted softly. They were placed delicately among threads of the spiders' silk.

"Isn't that the constellation of the Peacock's Treasure? And there's the Pouncing Tiger. You've made the night sky out of pearls!"

"We watch the ssstarsss and they tell usss many thingsss. They told usss of your quessst. They alssso told usss to help you reach the Jade Rabbit." The spider smiled.

"But how? Why?" The wee rabbit could hardly speak.

"Our waysss are not yoursss, Shhhabu. We do not know all, but we know thisss: you are on the right pathhh. Be patient. More ansssswersss will come sssoon enough."

The old spider stood. "Come Shhhabu. Come, King Ka Shhhoo. Under the Sssun, the Moon and the Sssky! Terribl foesss vanquishhhed! Monkeysss and ssspidersss as friendsss again! We have many, many wondersss to ccccelebrate."

Days later, it was time to go home.

Journal Entry 6

Leaving my new friends is not easy, but more adventures await. The spiders have agreed to give me all the silk thread I need and the monkeys have offered to weave it to cover the Lunar Venture Vessel. I'm taking some silk with me but the rest will be delivered to the Burrow soon. Poor Messenger Mice—it's a lot of silk! The Department of Postal Affairs will have a fit.

I finally understand Grandfather's long absences while I was growing up. The danger outside the Burrow is real but worth facing to meet such good friends. I miss them already.

Don't worry, Jade Rabbit, the first part of the ship will soon be completed.

I am on my way.

The Venture Vessel floated home in the moonlight.

"It's a bit chilly up here," Shabu thought.
She reached for a blanket to warm her. Under it, she spied
the end of an out-of-place metal handle. She gave a big
laugh. "I don't believe it... I found Chow's wrench!"

Thus concludes
Book 2

Join Shabu Shabu on her journey
to the Moon with

The Haunted Castle

where one may or may not find the
answers to these questions:

- How many Messenger Mice and
  Postal Pigeons will it take to deliver
  Shabu's silk?

- Will Shabu manage to return safely
  to the Burrow without crashing her
  balloon yet again?

- If she survives the journey home,
  will Shabu accidentally blow up the
  Burrow before Chow gets back from
  his family visit?

*To be
continued...*

❧ Credits ❧
Creators

Kristina Thornton
Words

Michael Csokas
Words/Pictures

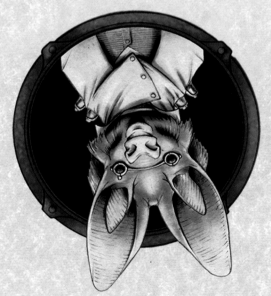

Ricardo Contreras
Color

Ola Olaniyi
Commerce

Title design by
Michelle McBri

Messenger Mouse 227 accepted a scroll from a bejeweled paw.

"The Queen is dangerous and may be angered by reading this, my dear little friend, so do not linger after the message has been delivered. I would not ask you to go on this mission if it was not of the utmost importance."

Books so far in the **The Wee Adventures of Shabu Shabu**
eight part series:

Book 1 The Jade legend

Book 2 The Silk Route

Book 3 The Haunted Castle
Coming soon